# Captain AWESOME
## VS THE EVIL BABYSITTER

By STAN KIRBY

Illustrated by GEORGE O'CONNOR

LITTLE SIMON

New York  London  Toronto  Sydney  New Delhi

LITTLE SIMON

An imprint of Simon & Schuster Children's Publishing Division • 1230 Avenue of the Americas, New York, New York 10020 • First Little Simon edition July 2014 • Copyright © 2014 by Simon & Schuster, Inc. All rights reserved, including the right of reproduction in whole or in part in any form. LITTLE SIMON is a registered trademark of Simon & Schuster, Inc., and associated colophon is a trademark of Simon & Schuster, Inc. For information about special discounts for bulk purchases, please contact Simon & Schuster Special Sales at 1-866-506-1949 or business@simonandschuster.com. The Simon & Schuster Speakers Bureau can bring authors to your live event. For more information or to book an event contact the Simon & Schuster Speakers Bureau at 1-866-248-3049 or visit our website at www.simonspeakers.com. Designed by Jay Colvin. The text of this book was set in Little Simon Gazette.
Manufactured in the United States of America 0614 FFG 10 9 8 7 6 5 4 3 2 1
Library of Congress Cataloging-in-Publication Data
Kirby, Stan. Captain Awesome vs. the evil babysitter / by Stan Kirby ; illustrated by George O'Connor. — First edition. pages cm. — (Captain Awesome ; #11) Summary: "When Eugene's parents go away for the weekend, he discovers that his babysitter is a true villain! Will Captain Awesome be able to save himself—and his little sister—from the evil babysitter?"— Provided by publisher. [1. Superheroes—Fiction. 2. Supervillains—Fiction. 3. Babysitters—Fiction.] I. O'Connor, George, illustrator. II. Title. III. Title: Captain Awesome versus the evil babysitter. PZ7.K633529Cb 2012 [Fic]—dc23 2013028256
ISBN 978-1-4814-0447-1 (hc)
ISBN 978-1-4814-0446-4 (pbk)
ISBN 978-1-4814-0448-8 (eBook)

# Table of Contents

# CHAPTER 1

## The Weekend of Greatness!

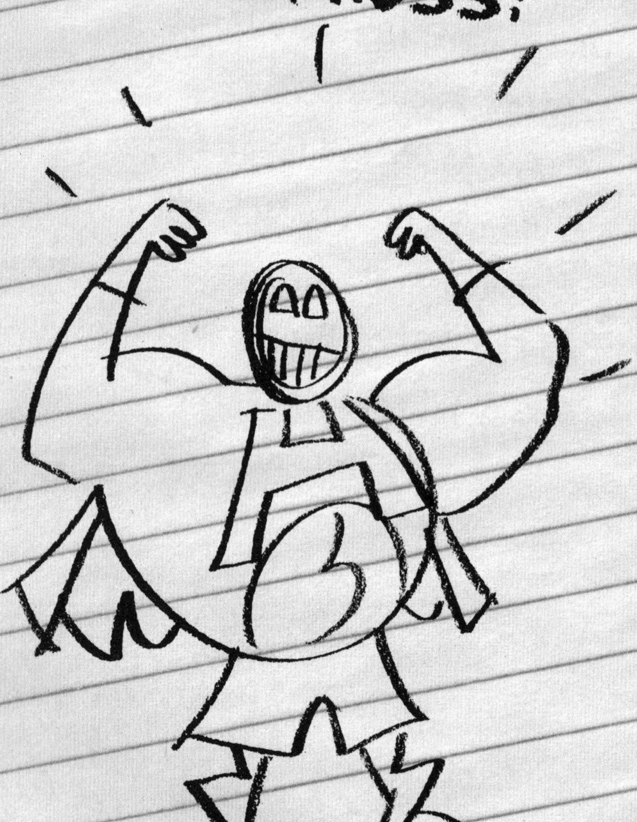

By
Eugene

# TICK, TOCK, TICK, TOCK.

Eugene stared at the clock on the wall as his second-grade teacher, Ms. Beasley, said lots of words he wasn't listening to. He had more important things to think about.

Like: Was the bell ever going ring?

And: What was taking the weekend so long to get here?

*I have big plans*, Eugene thought.
*Big weekend plans!*

## THE WEEKEND!

Eugene squirmed in his chair. He could hardly wait for it. Friday. Saturday. Sunday. Are there any three days that go together better?

They're like cake, icing, and sprinkles! They're like popping a balloon and finding it's full of ice cream! They're like, well, you get the idea.

Eugene scribbled in his notebook the top three things he loved most about weekends:

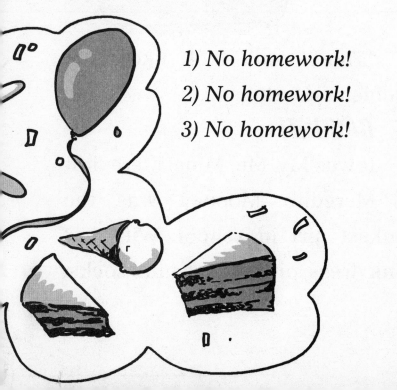

*1) No homework!*
*2) No homework!*
*3) No homework!*

"Those don't look like math problems, Dork-gene."

**CAUGHT!**

It was My. Me. Mine. Meredith!

Meredith Mooney was the pinkest girl in school. With her pink dress, pink shoes, pink socks,

and pink ribbons in her hair, she
was so pink that cotton candy was
jealous.

"It's nothing, Meredith." Eugene
quickly slid his list under his math
book. "Just my big plans for the
weekend."

"Ha. Big plans." She laughed. "Big *loser* plans is more like it."

She turned away, still laughing.

Eugene didn't care. Nothing was going to ruin his weekend.

*This is going to be the best weekend ever in the history of Friday, Saturday, and Sunday,* thought Eugene.

It was just like that story in

Super Dude No. 43, *Super Dude's Fun Time*, when Super Dude realized that every villain in the world was in jail and he could do whatever he wanted.

That was a good issue and—

**WHAT?**

You mean you don't know the world's greatest superhero? The one whose legendary adventures are chronicled in a series of every-word-is-true comic books?

**SHAME!**

Super Dude is the superhero who once kicked the snot out of Boogerman. He's the one who wiped the floor with Moppy Mopp's Dust Devils of Destruction.

He was also Eugene's favorite superhero of all time. Eugene was

so inspired by the adventures of
Super Dude that he created an
alter ego of his own and became
Sunnyview's first superhero . . .
CAPTAIN AWESOME!

*MI-TEE!*

But evil never rests, and that's

more than one superhero boy can handle by himself. That's why Eugene was joined by his best friends, Charlie Thomas Jones and Sally Williams. Together, with their class pet hamster, Turbo, they were the Sunnyview Superhero Squad.

Charlie became Nacho Cheese Man—the only hero with the power of canned cheese!

*CHEESY YO!*

And Sally? She was Supersonic Sal—faster than the speed of light!

*SPEEDY GO!*

These four heroes put badness

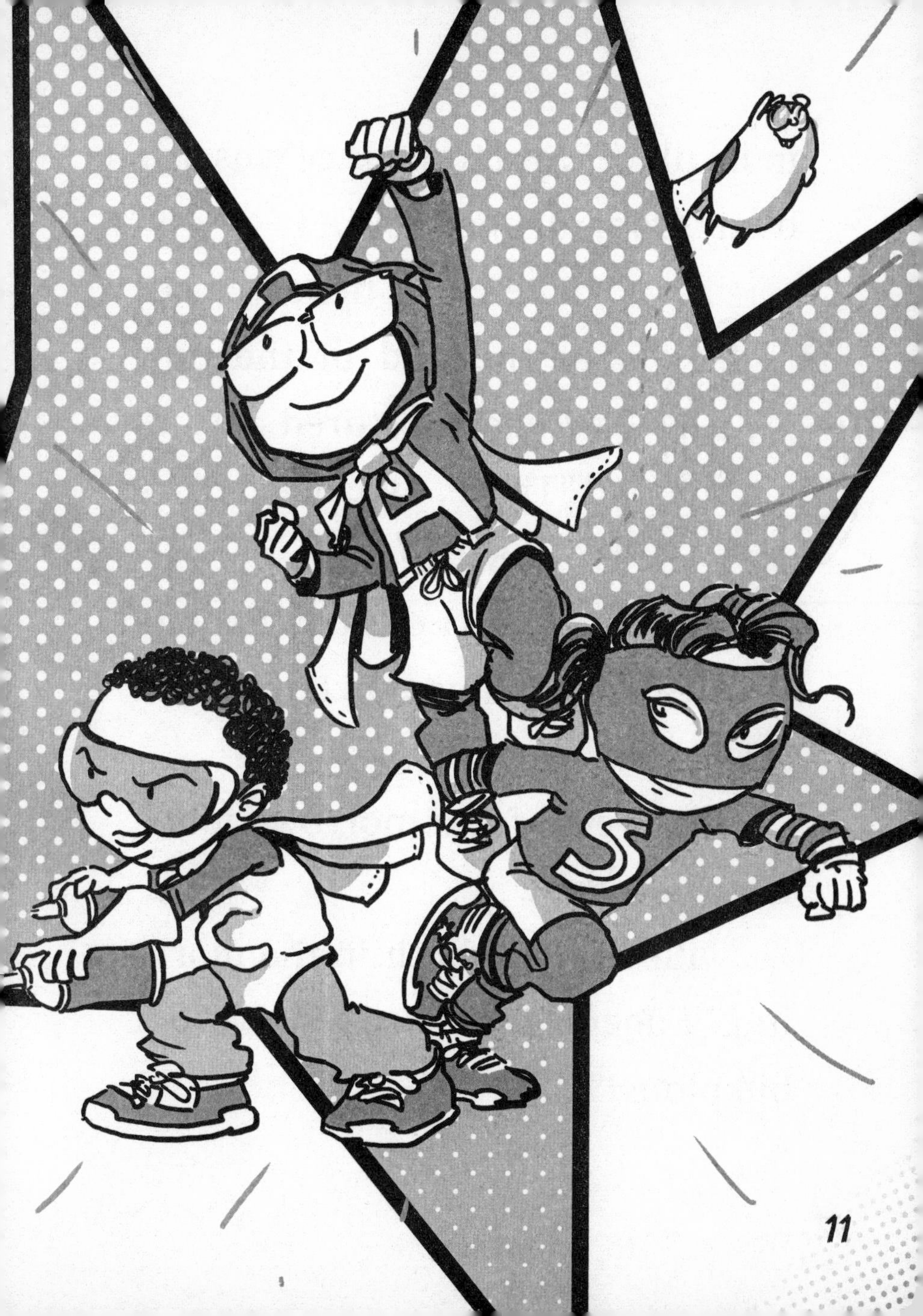

in its place! And that place was: far away from all goodness.

 The clock ticked closer to the end of the day. Eugene stared at it: "Three, two, one . . ."

## *RING!*

"Yes! Let's go!" Eugene yelled as the students burst from the school.

"We're on for tomorrow, right?" Charlie asked.

"I'll call you both in the morning," Eugene promised. "We've got big plans!"

"Bike riding!" Sally said.

"Hide-and-seek!" Charlie cried.

"Evil-fighting!" Eugene yelled.

It was going to be a *great* weekend.

# CHAPTER 2

# A Change of Plans

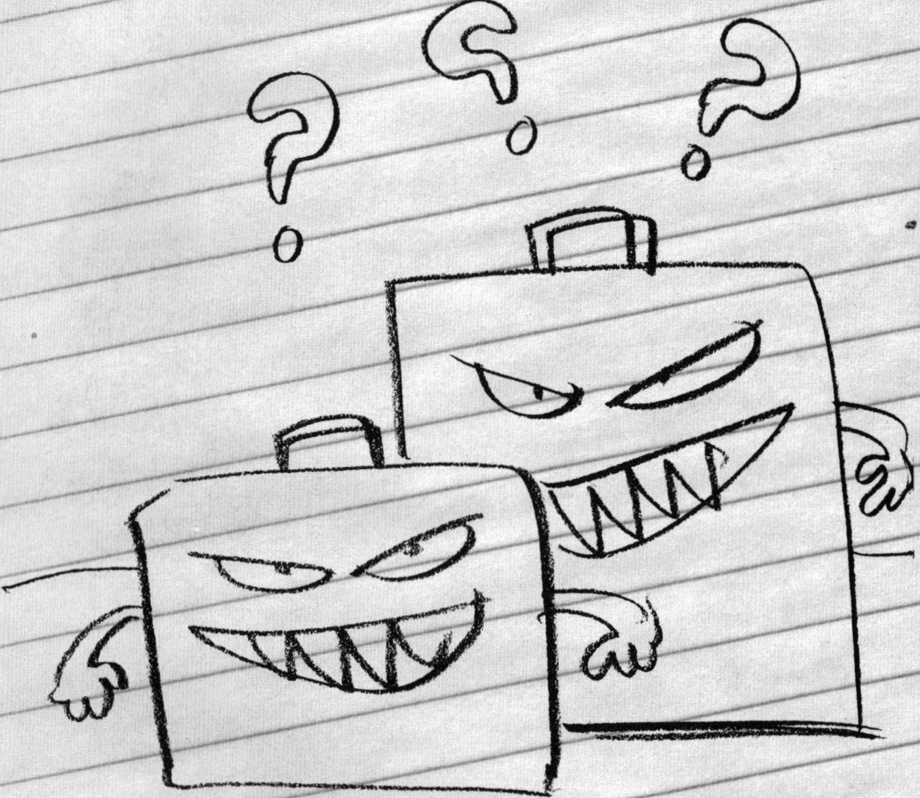

By
Eugene

"**Yes!**" Saturday morning was here, and Eugene shot out of bed like a clown from a circus cannon. "Saturday! Saturday! Saturday!"he sang as he danced down the stairs. "Hello, weekend! So very glad to see you!"

It was time for a breakfast of Super Dude's Flakes & Fiber cereal, and then a meeting with Sally and Charlie to get this weekend started.

Sometimes, though, no matter how much you plan for something, evil hits you right in the guts—so hard that you see double.

Eugene saw double by the front door.

Two suitcases.

"Hey, Mom!" he called to the kitchen. "Did you and Dad pack early for next weekend's trip?"

"The trip is *this* weekend, honey," Mrs. McGillicudy replied. "Your father and I leave for the Cherry Computers conference in just a few minutes."

GASP!

*No! This can't be true*, Eugene thought.

"We talked about this all week," Eugene's mom reminded him.

*Oh sure,* Eugene thought. *I'll bet they tried to tell me while I was reading Super Dude comics or watching TV or trying to figure out when evil Commander Barfing Barfington was going to hurl over the city again.*

"But I thought Aunt Beatrice was coming next weekend? You know, like, *next* Saturday."

"Oh, that's the other thing. Aunt Beatrice injured herself opening a can of Spam. Her replacement should be here any minute."

"Replacement? Who could replace Aunt Beatrice?" Eugene asked.

## DING-DONG!

The doorbell rang. "That should be the babysitter now," his mom said.

Babysitter?!

## SHOCK!
## HORROR!

"She'll take very good care of you and Molly while your father and I are gone."

"A *babysitter*?" Eugene protested. "Really, Mom? I'm in second grade. I can take care of myself!"

A surprise babysitter was like having a substitute teacher who didn't know that they should *never* give a pop quiz.

Mrs. McGillicudy reached out for the doorknob. Eugene shifted his feet nervously. The mystery sitter was waiting behind that door.

*And he or she is about to ruin my weekend!* thought Eugene.

The door creaked open. . . .

## CHAPTER 3

# The Sitter of Doom

By Eugene

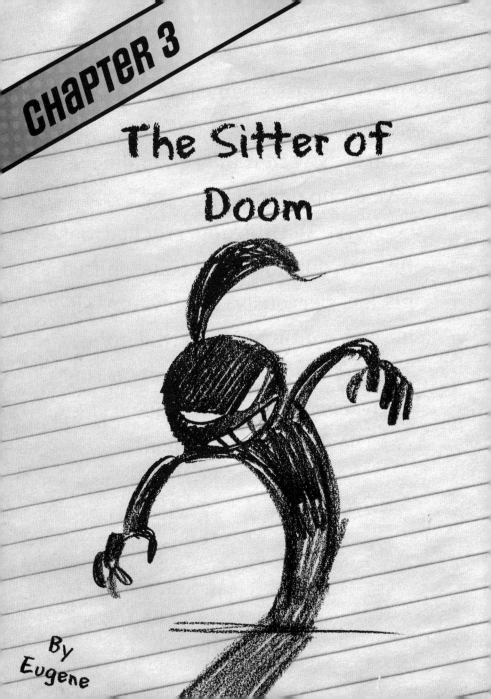

"**G**ood morning, Mr. and Mrs. McGillicudy!"

"Hello!" Eugene's mother said. "Eugene, this is Melissa."

Melissa was tall with long blond hair the color of the Sun-burner, the Fourth Earl of Sunbeam, the supervillain who stole the moon in Super Dude No. 82. She wore that hair in a ponytail that bounced when she moved her head. To Eugene, she might as well have been wearing a steel mask, carrying a samurai sword, and petting a shark with laser eyes.

"Hi, Melissa," Eugene said with a grumble.

Eugene's dad came in carrying Molly. "She's all changed and good for at least a couple of hours. Maybe."

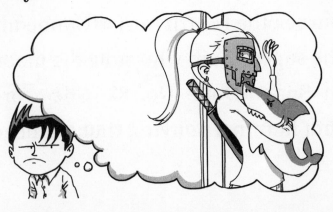

Melissa took Eugene's little sister. Eugene's mom and dad both kissed Molly good-bye and each gave Eugene a big hug.

"Be nice and help out Melissa, okay? We'll see you Sunday night."

Eugene's dad picked up the suitcases and headed to the car. "Right on schedule," he said.

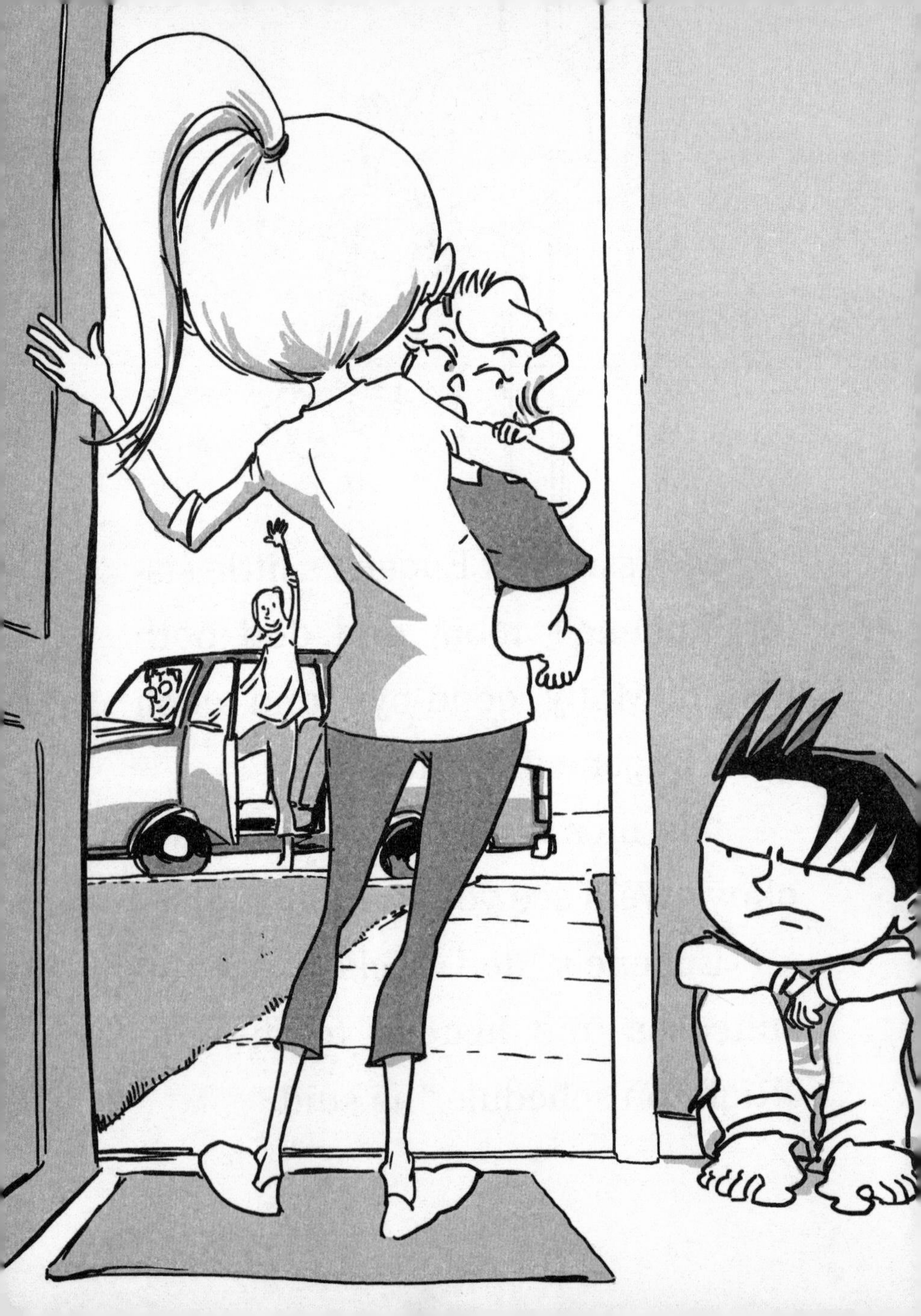

Mrs. McGillicudy paused by the front door. "Don't hesitate to call if you need anything," she said to Melissa. "If you want pizza, call Buchsbaum's. They deliver. And if the power goes out, call the electric company. And if any zombies show up, well, I don't know who to call about that. And—"

"Mrs. McGillicudy, I think I've got it," Melissa said. "Have a great time at the conference."

Eugene looked out the open door. The sky was blue. There was a gentle breeze. The grass was wet from the morning dew.

*At least I can still hang out with my friends*, thought Eugene.

"I think we're going to have a lot of fun, Eugene," Melissa said. "I have only one rule."

*Only one rule?* Eugene liked the sound of that. *Will it be "Ice cream*

all day?" he wondered. Or "TV all day?" Or "You can play with your friends all day?"

"My only rule is that you must stay in the house or play in the yard all day. No going to anyone else's house either."

## WHAT?!

"You can get started on  your homework or clear the breakfast dishes." Melissa's voice sounded like the scratch of monster nails on Dr. Frankenstein's chalkboard. "Your call. I think I need to change your baby sister because something around here really smells, and I don't think it's you or me. Be right back."

**SIGH.**

*I've got to figure out a way to contact Charlie and Sally,* he thought. *They're counting on me.*

But how?

# CHAPTER 4

## Can You Hear Me Now? How About Now?

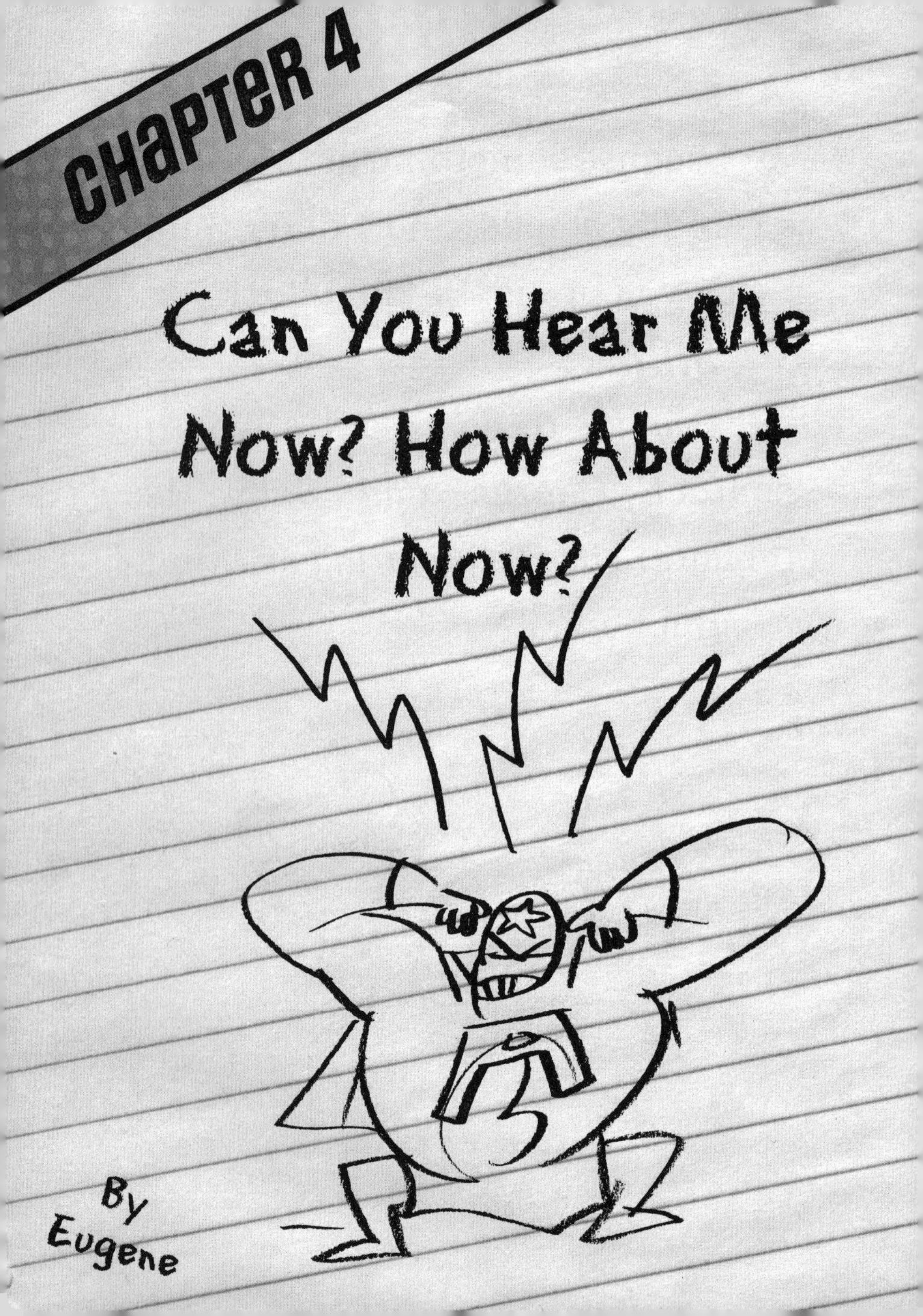
By
Eugene

**F**lashlight signals! Nope, it was light out. Carrier pigeon! Nope, Eugene didn't have one. Carrier *hamster!*

*I could tie a note to Turbo and . . .*

Eugene raced up to his room to check on Turbo. But the hamster was fast asleep in his wheel. Was he snoring?

*Must think of something else!*

THINK! That's it. Thinking!

He could use Captain Awesome's amazing mental powers of telepathy to send a message to his friends.

Eugene stood as still as a piece of toast that had landed jelly-side down on the floor. He clenched his hands and closed his eyes.

"By the awesome power of

Captain Awesome's mighty brain energy, I call the magnificent mind beams to the front of my head."

**BEAM!**

**BEAM-BEAM!**

Eugene was supersure he felt a tingle on his forehead.

*Sally, Charlie, this is Eugene,* Eugene thought-beamed. *Babysitter. Trapped. Weekend in jeopardy. If you can hear me . . .*

He opened one eye.

Nothing.

Then the other eye. Still nothing. He might as well be invisible.

Wait! Invisible! That was it!

"I'll use Captain Awesome's 'Can't-See-Me' Powers of Invisibility." He grabbed his superhero cape.

"Oh, Awesome Cape, hear my wish, make me as invisible as . . . an invisible fish!"

**_BAM!_**
**_DONE!_**

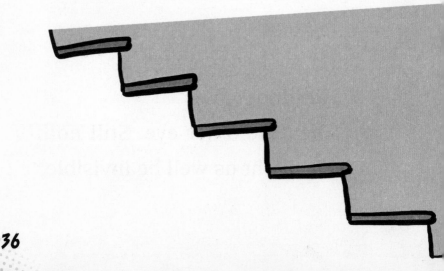

Invisible Eugene walked downstairs to the front door. No need to hide because no one, not even a babysitter, could see him. If he hurried, he could make it to Charlie's house and back without being missed . . . or seen!

He turned the knob on the front door.

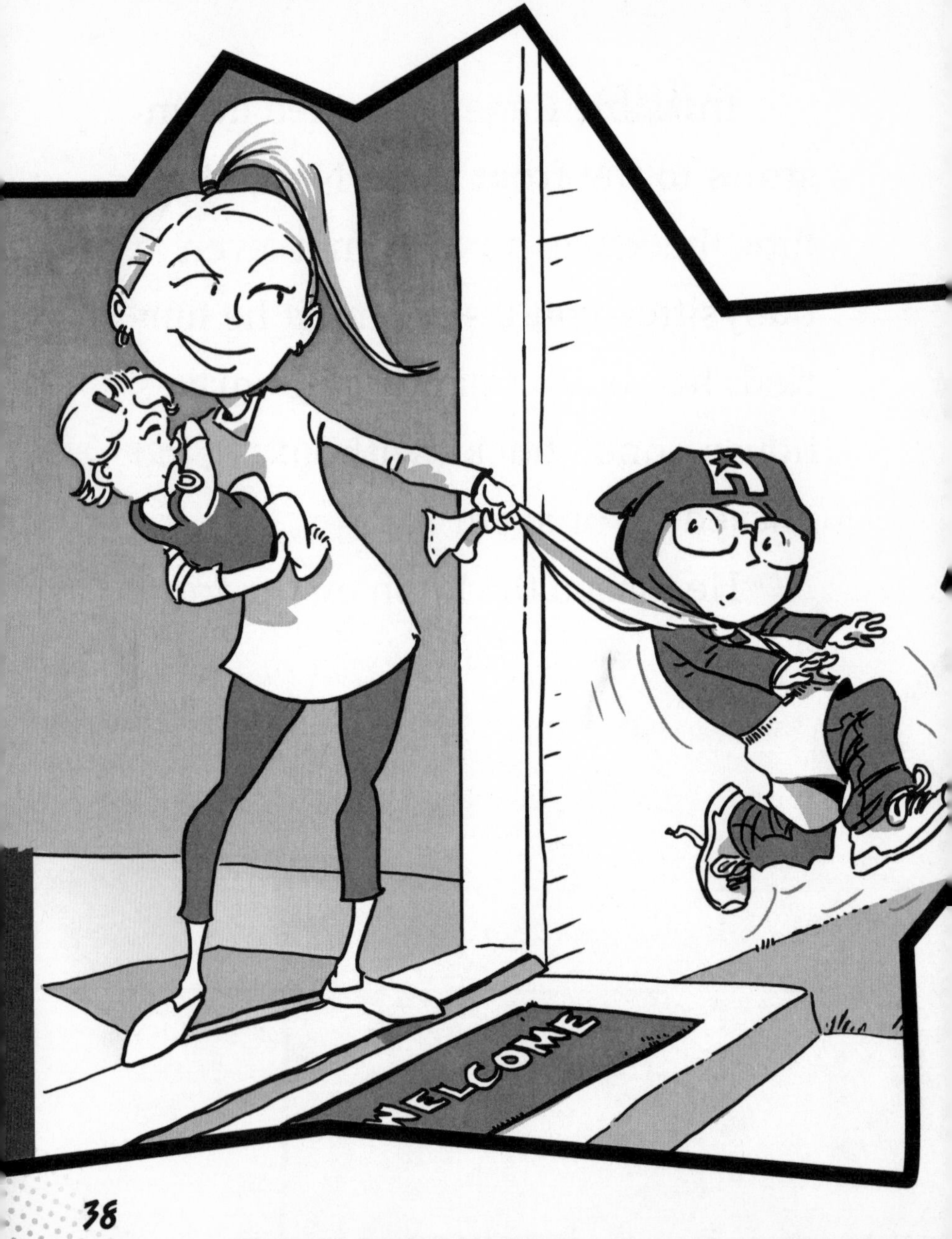
WELCOME

**SQUEAK.**

Melissa came in carrying Molly. "Where are you going?"

"But— But— But," Eugene stuttered like a motorboat engine. "I need . . . I mean . . . I'm supposed to see Charlie and Sally for . . . a secret meeting. No! I mean, to do . . . homework together," he said.

"No can do. You know my rule: stay in the yard," Melissa said, wagging a finger at him. "Now do me a favor and watch Molly. I promised your mom I'd do some chores around the house," she added.

Melissa disappeared into the laundry room, leaving Eugene alone with Molly. But this was no ordinary diaper-human—oh, no. Molly was really one of Captain Awesome's truly evil enemies, the dreaded Queen Stinkypants from Planet Baby.

And she was at it again! In her grabby little hand she held Eugene's rare Super Dude action figure with

Dude-Jitsu action awesomeness. She put the head in her mouth, ready to bite it.

If ever there was a time for Captain Awesome, this was it!

"Queen Stinkypants!" yelled Captain Awesome. "Leave the precious brains of Super Dude inside his own head!"

Captain Awesome took one step forward, tripped on Queen Stinkypants's rubber ball of evil, and fell to the ground.

**_WHAM!_**

The rubber ball shot across the room. As it zoomed past Queen Stinkypants, she dropped Super Dude and chased after it.

*The rulers of Planet Baby are easily distracted by new things. Mission accomplished!* Eugene thought as he picked up the Super Dude action figure. He also got a handful of evil drool.

**GROSS!**

# CHAPTER 5

# The Most Evil Lunch Ever

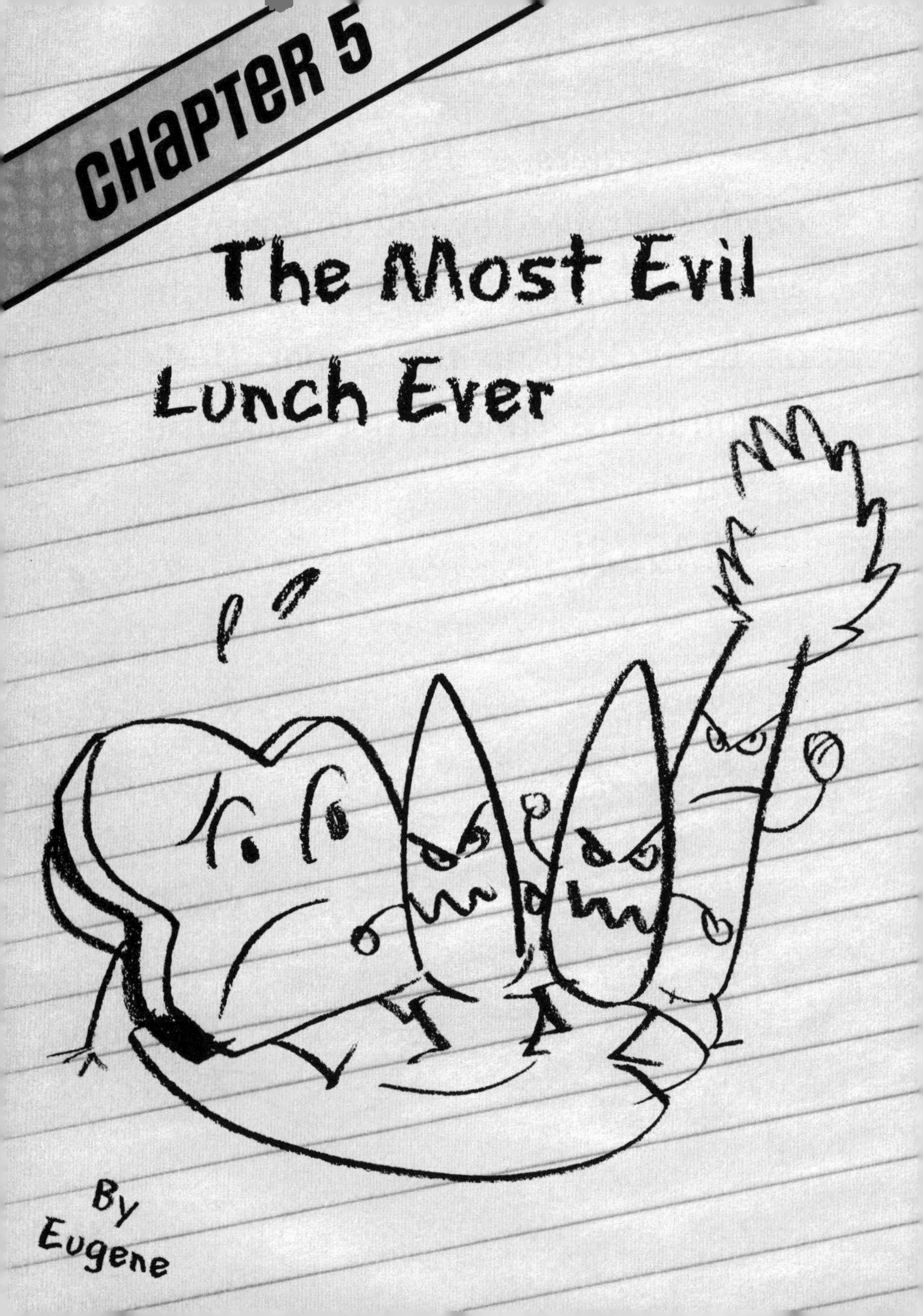

By Eugene

"Lunch is ready!" Melissa set a plate on the kitchen table for Eugene. He looked down and saw the sweet deliciousness of peanut butter and jelly, pressed together between two pieces of bread.

"Excuse me, Melissa," Eugene said. "What's this other stuff on my plate?"

"Those are carrots and celery sticks," she said.

## GROSS!

"My mom usually gives me a chocolate chip cookie at lunch," Eugene said.

Melissa joined him at the table with her own sandwich. "You can have *one* cookie for dessert. When you finish everything on your plate."

For a babysitter with only one rule, she sure has a lot of others, Eugene thought.

"You know, my little sister is in your class," Melissa said.

"Mooth yoor ittle ister?" Eugene asked, his mouth packed full with peanut butter.

"My sister is Meredith."

*Hmmmmmm*, thought Eugene. *Maybe there's a new Meredith in class because the only Meredith I know is . . .*

## NO! WHAT? NO!

Eugene's brain couldn't process this. If there were a door in his

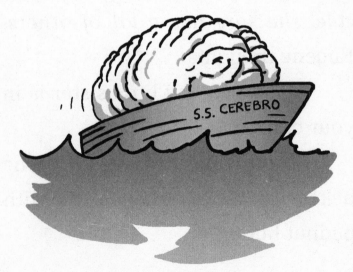

head, his brain would have opened it, hopped to the Sunnyview Pier, and thrown itself onto the first boat to Tanzania.

"Your sister is . . . Meredith Mooney?" Eugene asked. "My . . . Me . . . Mine . . . MERE-dith?!"

Eugene could barely speak. Words were jammed in his throat. "Could I eat on the porch? I need some air."

"Okay," Melissa said. "But just remember my rule: Don't leave the yard."

Outside, Eugene sat on the steps, his mind racing. *I can't go anywhere,* he thought. *I'm trapped. How do*

*prisoners ever get in touch with their friends?*

## HOW?

Eugene looked up and saw Sally. She was down the street, getting her bike out of the garage. Perfect. Now he just had to get her attention.

Eugene started to step off the

porch but stopped, mid-step. What if Melissa put up a force field to keep him in the yard? *That's just what she'd do*, he thought.

But then he thought again: *No force field could ever stop Captain Awesome!*

**MI-TEE!**

Captain Awesome leaped from the porch at full power. He put his hands out in front and his head down, and burst from the yard to the fresh air of freedom and sidewalks!

"Sally Williams!" called out Captain Awesome. "You're never going to believe who has a sister!"

After Eugene told her the evil details, Sally was shocked.

"Captain Awesome being held prisoner?" she said. "The Sunnyview Superhero Squad will have something to say about this."

Captain Awesome smiled. "It's good to have friends!"

"I'll get Charlie, and we'll come back to rescue you." Sally turned her bicycle around, about to head back to her house. Then she stopped. "What will you do?"

"I have to sneak back into the house so the evil babysitter doesn't suspect anything." Eugene crept inside. He had to be careful. If Melissa had seen him talking to Sally, then all hope was lost. She'd throw him into some playpen prison until he was old enough to drive a car . . . which was in, like, ten thousand years.

Melissa sat on the couch, watching TV. Step-by-step Eugene tiptoed past the living room. If he could just get to the stairs, all would be well. He moved slower than the Slimy Slugs of Icktopia.

*Almost there ... Almost there ... Almost ...*

"Who was that you were talking to?"

AAAAAARRRRRRRRRRRGH!

Eugene was so close it actually hurt when he heard Melissa's voice. Maybe if he didn't move . . . didn't breathe . . . didn't blink . . . Melissa would think he didn't hear her and he could—

"Don't pretend you didn't hear me," she said without even turning around to look.

DOUBLE AAAAAARRRRGH!

She knew his every trick!

*How could I have been so care-
less?! Eugene thought. Of course,
she has Babysitter Radar! She can
sense any sneaking kid within one
hundred feet!*

"It was just my very ordinary

and non-superhero friend Sally," Eugene answered. "We were talking about very boring things that have nothing to do with breaking out of evil prisons."

"Well, no play dates on *my* watch," Melissa said. "Which reminds me, you're supposed to clean your room."

"But Mom and Dad only make me clean my room on Sundays!"

Eugene protested. "And today's *not* Sunday!"

Eugene stared at the back of Melissa's head. She sat like a

TV-watching statue with blond hair, pretending to not hear Eugene.

*She's using my own "I didn't hear you" trick against me!* Eugene thought. *That is so unfair!*

# CHAPTER 6

# Beware the Stinky Sock!

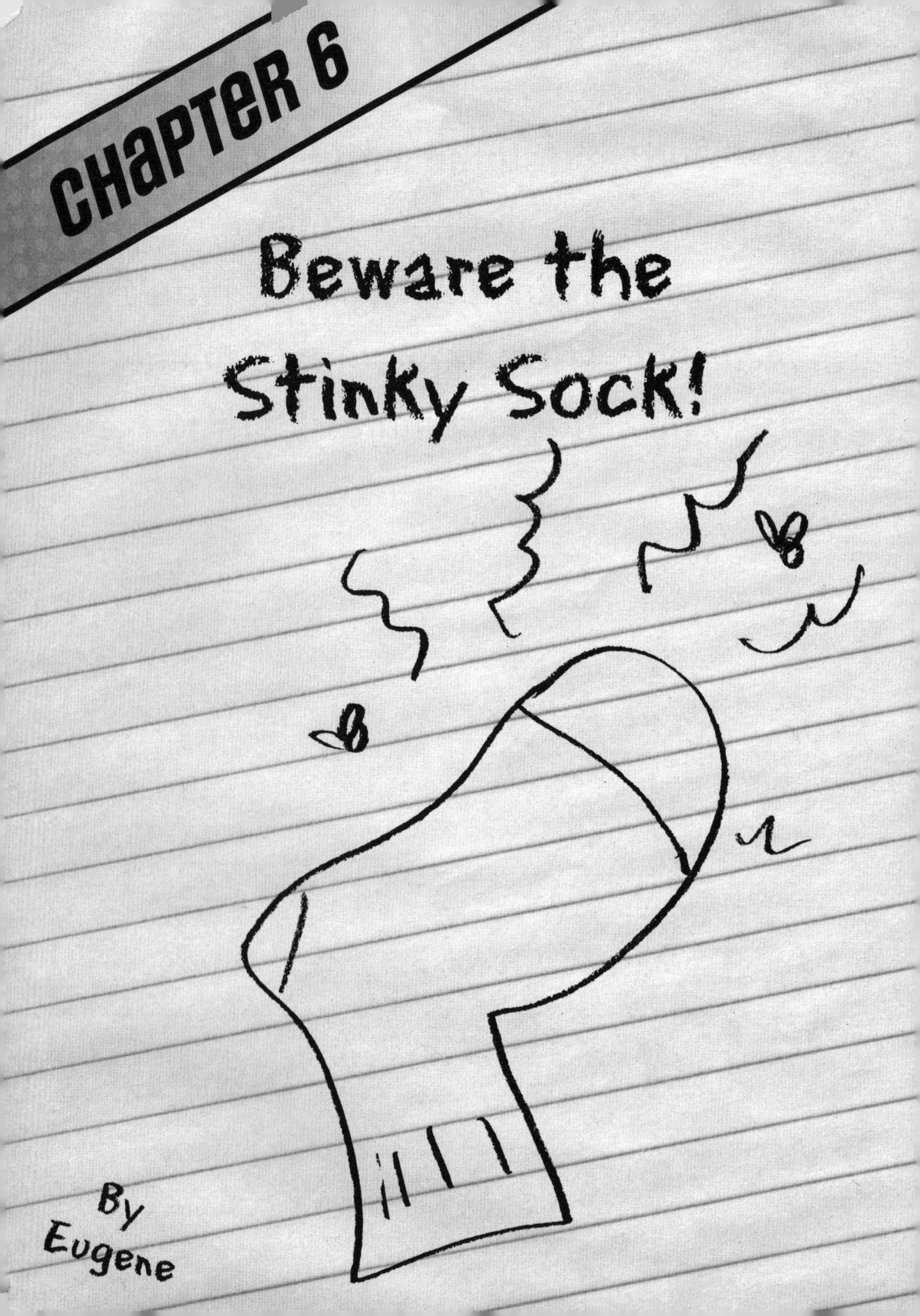

By
Eugene

Eugene sat on the floor of his room. At least he *thought* his floor was there somewhere, because he couldn't see an inch of it under all the clothes, toys, and Super Dude comics that covered the carpet.

Eugene picked up a sock and stared at it as if it had three eyes.

**PLINK!**

Eugene froze.

**PLINK!**

There it was again! Someone

was "plinking" him. But who? Or what?

**PLINK!**
**PLINK!**

It was coming from the window! Eugene leaped up and looked out. Peeking out of the bushes in his backyard were Sally and Charlie, fully dressed in their superhero gear as Supersonic Sal and Nacho Cheese Man!

Eugene immediately lifted a finger to his lips to shush them. If Melissa heard them, she'd make him clean up his room *and* his little

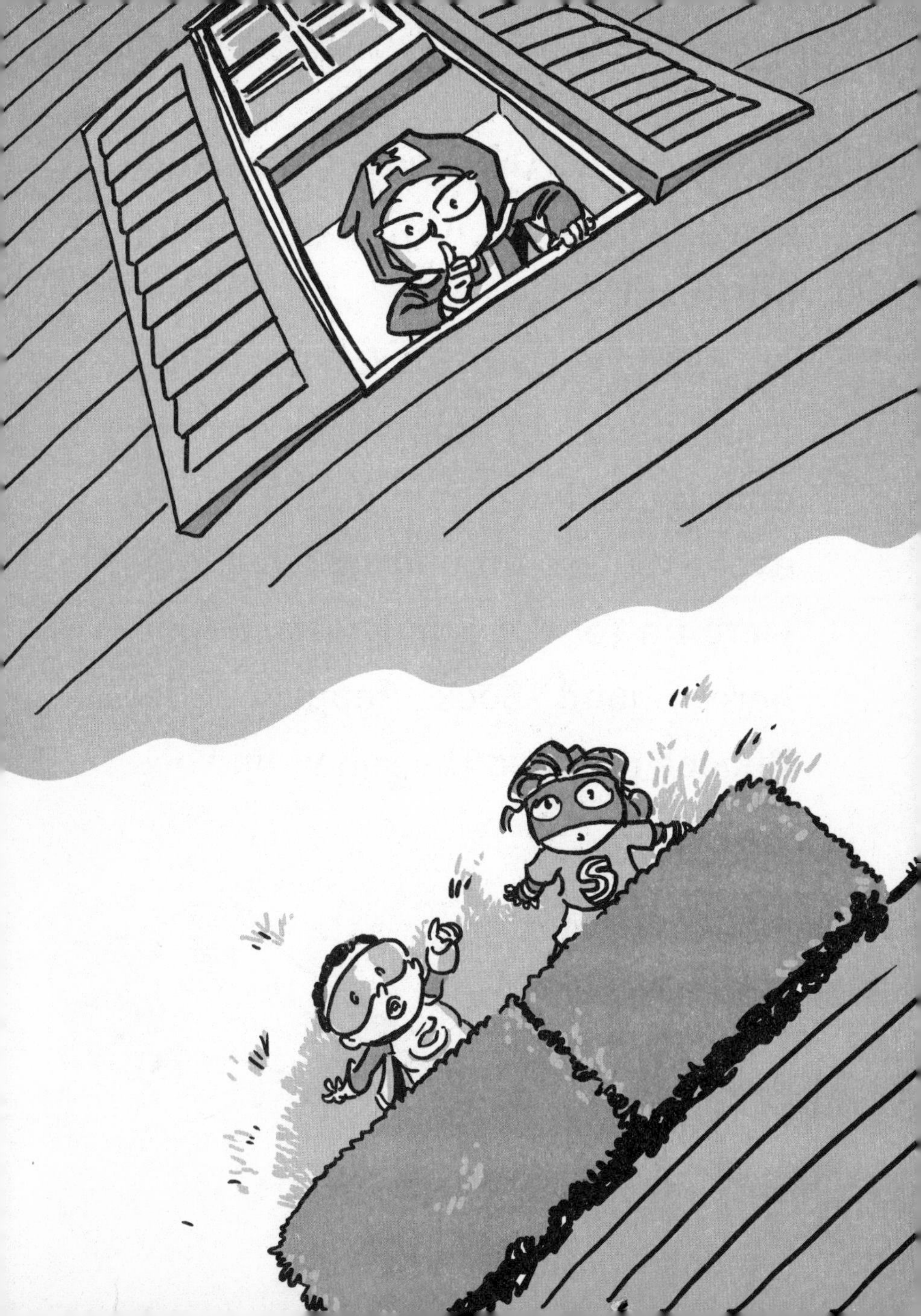

sister's. And that would make an already barfy day even more barftastic.

They needed a plan to break Eugene out of babysitter prison, and there was only one way to avoid Melissa finding out what they were up to: the Sunnyview Super-hero Squad Sock Puppet Code! Eugene grabbed the rolled-up sock

from the floor and slipped it over his hand.

## STINK!

Putting a week-old dirty sock over his hand was *not* a good idea. *This smells worse than the armpits of Major Sweat from Super Dude No. 12!*

Despite the awful smell of his own left sock, Eugene stood in front of the window and began the Sunnyview Superhero Squad Sock Puppet Code.

"What's he saying?" Supersonic Sal asked Nacho Cheese Man as

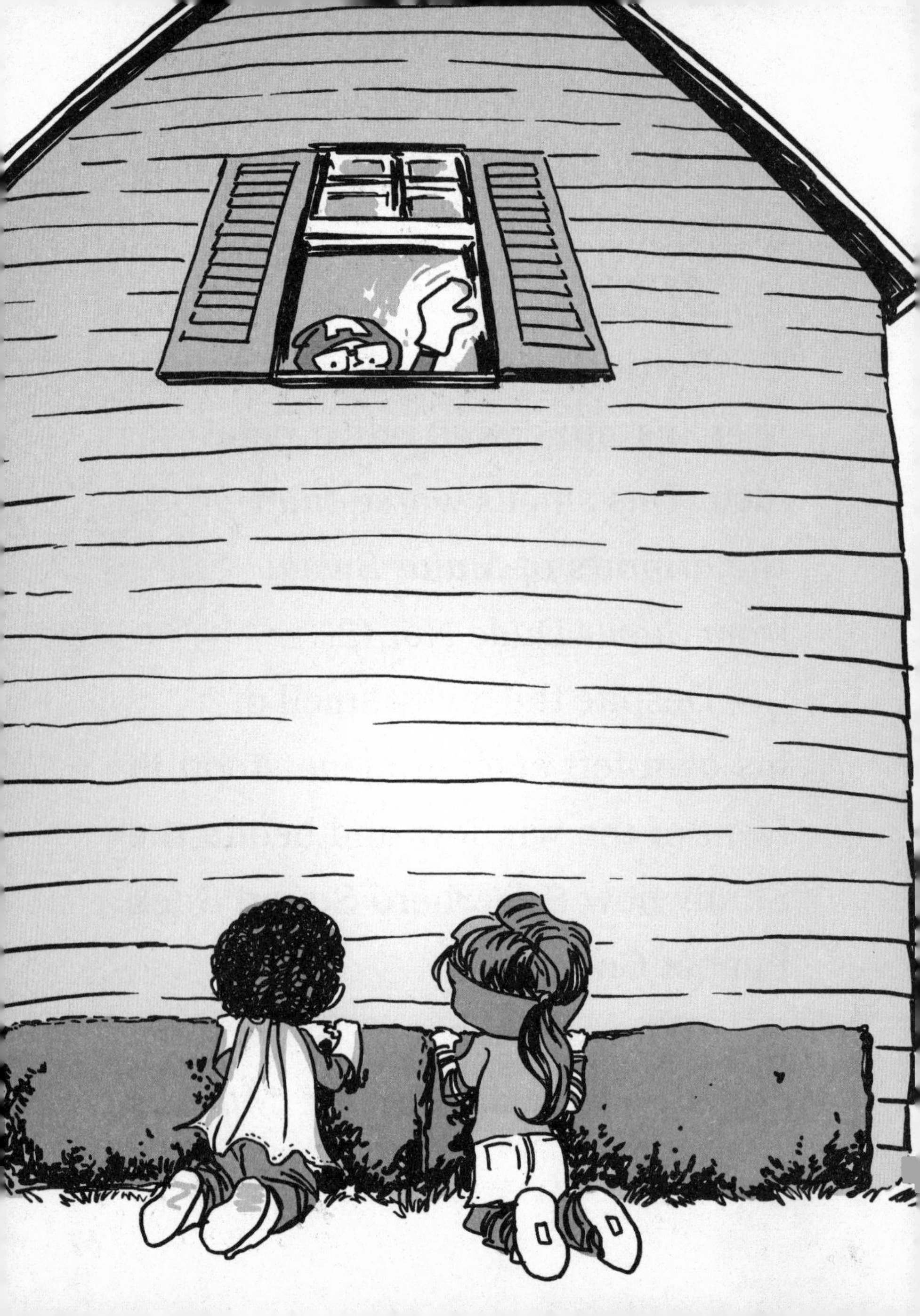

she watched Eugene open and close his hand to make the sock puppet's mouth move.

"Hold on a sec," Nacho Cheese Man replied. "Got . . . to . . . concentrate! Yes! Yes! I've got it!" Nacho Cheese Man turned to Supersonic Sal. "He's either saying 'We need a potato to get me out of this tuna fish' or 'This sock has three eyes.'"

"I don't think he's trying to tell us either one of those things," said Supersonic Sal.

"I probably should have paid more attention to Eugene when he explained the Sunnyview Super-hero Squad Sock Puppet Code to me." Nacho Cheese Man sighed.

A hopeful Eugene watched Nacho Cheese Man shrug.

"I knew Charlie should have paid more attention when I explained the Sunnyview Super-hero Squad Sock Puppet Code to him." Eugene sighed.

He looked around the room. There must be something there he could use to escape.

*I could put underwear over my head and tell Melissa that it attacked me!*

Eugene grabbed a pair of underwear from his drawer and stuck it on his head like a white, stretchy hat. And then Eugene had

an idea that was even *better* than wearing underwear on his head . . . although, just barely. He raced to his double secret stash of comic books.

"Behold! The answer to all my problems!" Eugene declared, and thrust a comic book into the air.

It was Super Dude No. 129. The one where Super Dude gets captured by the evil Dr. Chore and is forced to make all the lava beds on Volcania. But Super Dude manages to send out

a smoke signal to the Halloweenies,
and they defeat Dr. Chore with a
trick-or-treat attack.

"What's he doing?" Nacho
Cheese Man asked the moment he
saw Eugene slide his bedroom
window open. "It looks like he's
going to throw a—"

**SMACK!**

Super Dude No. 129 bonked Nacho Cheese Man on the head.

"I think that rotten babysitter sucked out Eugene's brain and replaced it with pudding!" Nacho Cheese Man said, picking up the comic. "Why would Eugene throw down Super Dude No. 129?"

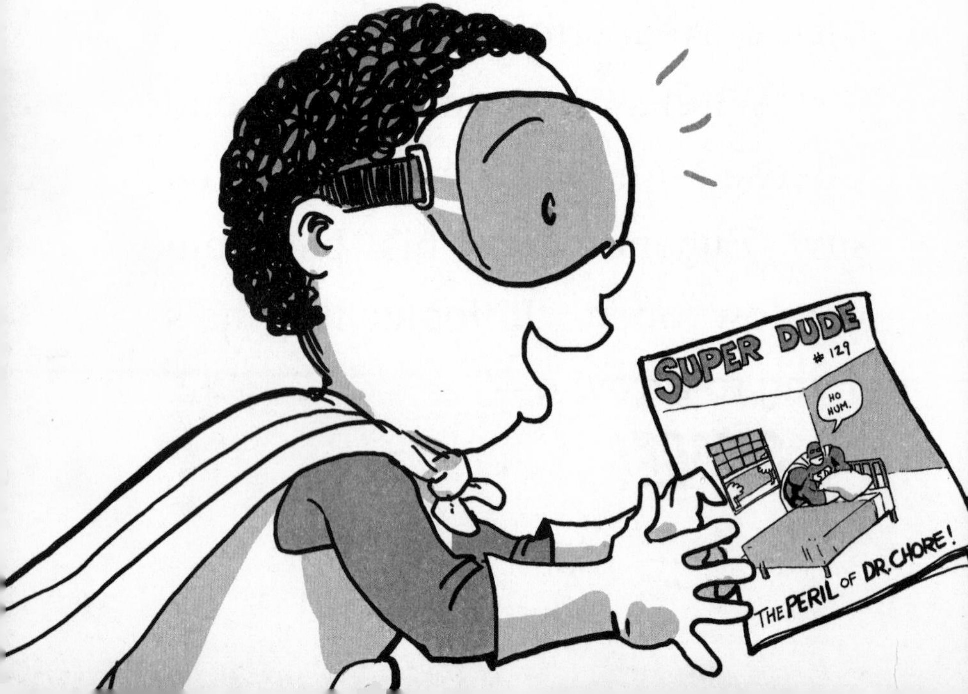
SUPER DUDE
# 129
HO HUM.
THE PERIL OF DR. CHORE!

"THE HALLOWEENIE TRICK-OR-TREAT ATTACK!" said Nacho Cheese Man and Supersonic Sal in unison as they both remembered what happens in No. 129.

"It's nowhere near Halloween," Supersonic Sal said. "A trick-or-treat

attack is the last thing Eugene's babysitter would expect!"

They gave the Sunnyview Superhero Squad Salute to Eugene and raced around the house to the front door.

Relieved, Eugene plopped back onto his bed. *Finally.* They had figured out the plan. But now was not the time for rest. The battle for his freedom was about to start. *Now* was the time for Captain Awesome.

**MI-TEE!**

# CHAPTER 7

## Popcorned!

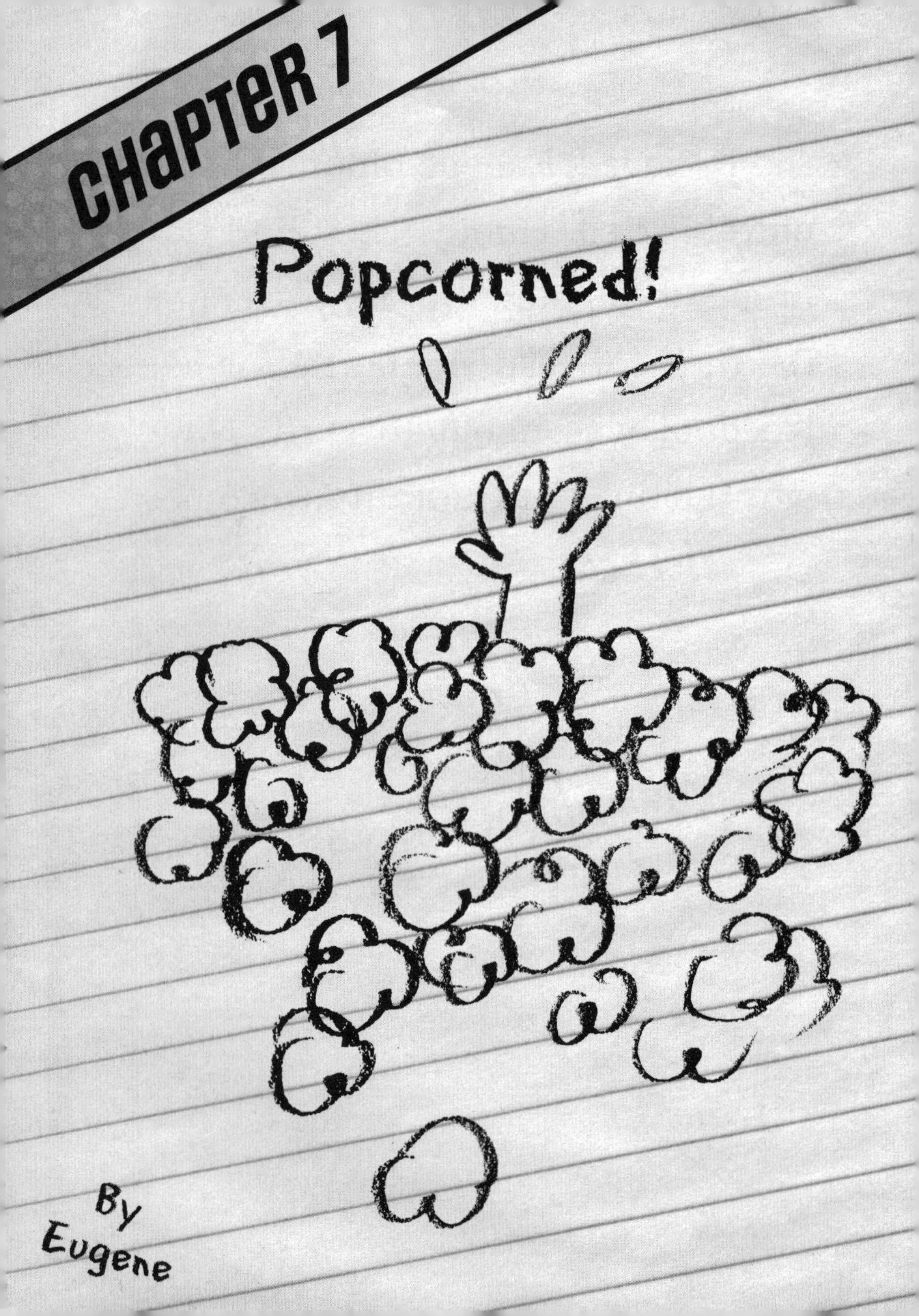

By
Eugene

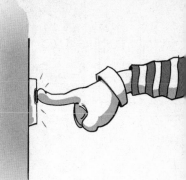

# Ding-dong!

Usually that was *just* the sound of the front doorbell, but today it was the ring of battle . . . and also the front doorbell.

Melissa looked through the peephole, a large bowl of freshly popped popcorn in her hand. She opened the door.

"Trick-or-treat!" the two heroes called out in unison. They hoped to

distract Melissa long enough for Eugene to make his escape out the back door.

"Trick-or-treat?" Melissa asked, confused. "But Halloween isn't for six months."

"She's on to us! Plan B! Plan B!" Nacho Cheese Man shouted in a panic.

"Nacho Cheese Man, there is no 'Plan B!'" Supersonic Sal replied.

"There is now!" Nacho Cheese Man whipped out two cans of cheese and sprayed Melissa.

"Hey! What are you doing?!" Melissa yelled.

Melissa staggered back from the open door, covered in spray cheese. Supersonic Sal raced past the confused babysitter and up the stairs, where she nearly collided with Captain Awesome, who was running in the opposite direction.

"We've launched 'Plan B!'" Supersonic Sal happily reported.

"What's 'Plan B?'" Captain Awesome asked.

"I'm not sure, exactly, but it seems to be working," Supersonic Sal replied.

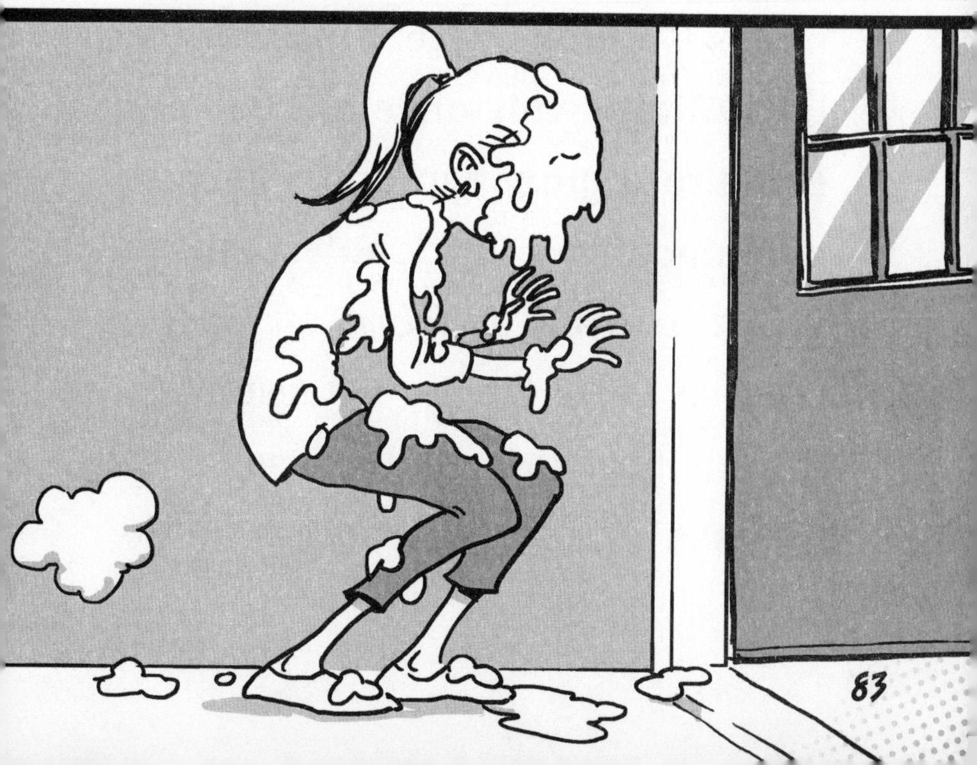

And it *was* working until the two heroes heard the shattering cry of "AAAAAAAAAAAAARGH! I'VE BEEN POPCORNED!"

Captain Awesome and Supersonic Sal rushed down the stairs, and what they saw sent their heads spinning like Topsy Turvy, the villain who once tied Super Dude to a giant top and sent him spinning into a black hole. Melissa was throwing popcorn at Nacho Cheese Man. Nacho Cheese Man did his best to shield himself, but Melissa's popcorn attack was too

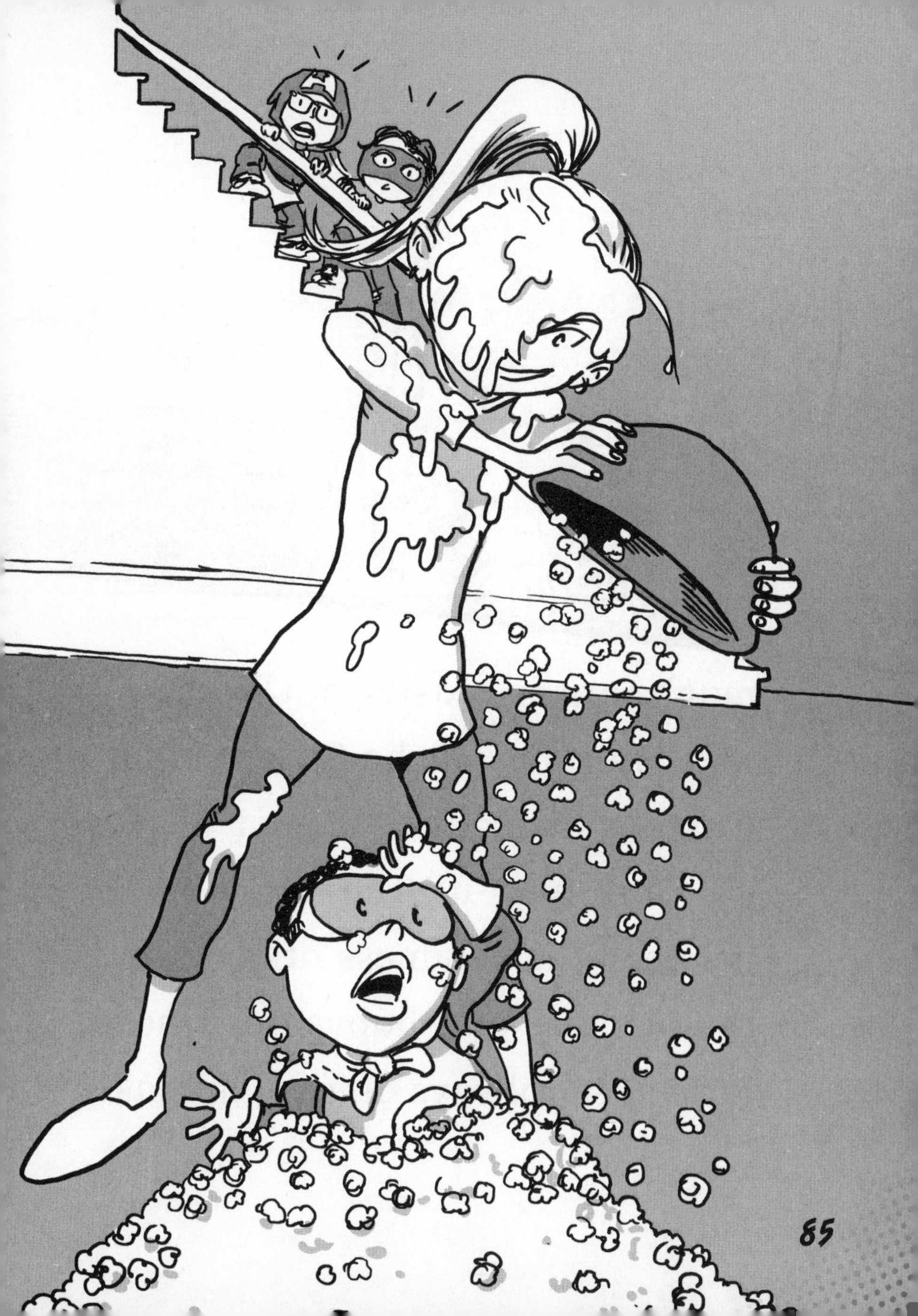

much for the Master of Cheese.

"Hang on, Nacho Cheese Man!"
Captain Awesome cried out.

This was it! The final battle
between the goodness of good and
the badness of a babysitter whose
little sister always dressed in pink!

Captain Awesome grabbed a
pot of spaghetti from the kitchen.
Supersonic Sal snatched up a bowl
of salad. "In the name of the Sunnyview Superhero Squad, I command
you to drop that popcorn!" cried
Captain Awesome.

"Oh, yeah?" Melissa said, turning to face Captain Awesome. "Well, I command you to EAT POPCORN!"

Then Melissa pelted Captain Awesome with a handful of popcorn.

**SALAD!**

Supersonic Sal threw a handful of lettuce and tomato slices at Melissa. Nacho Cheese Man jumped to his feet and rejoined the battle.

**SLOP!**
**PLOP!**
**SQUIRT!**
**SPAGHETTI!**

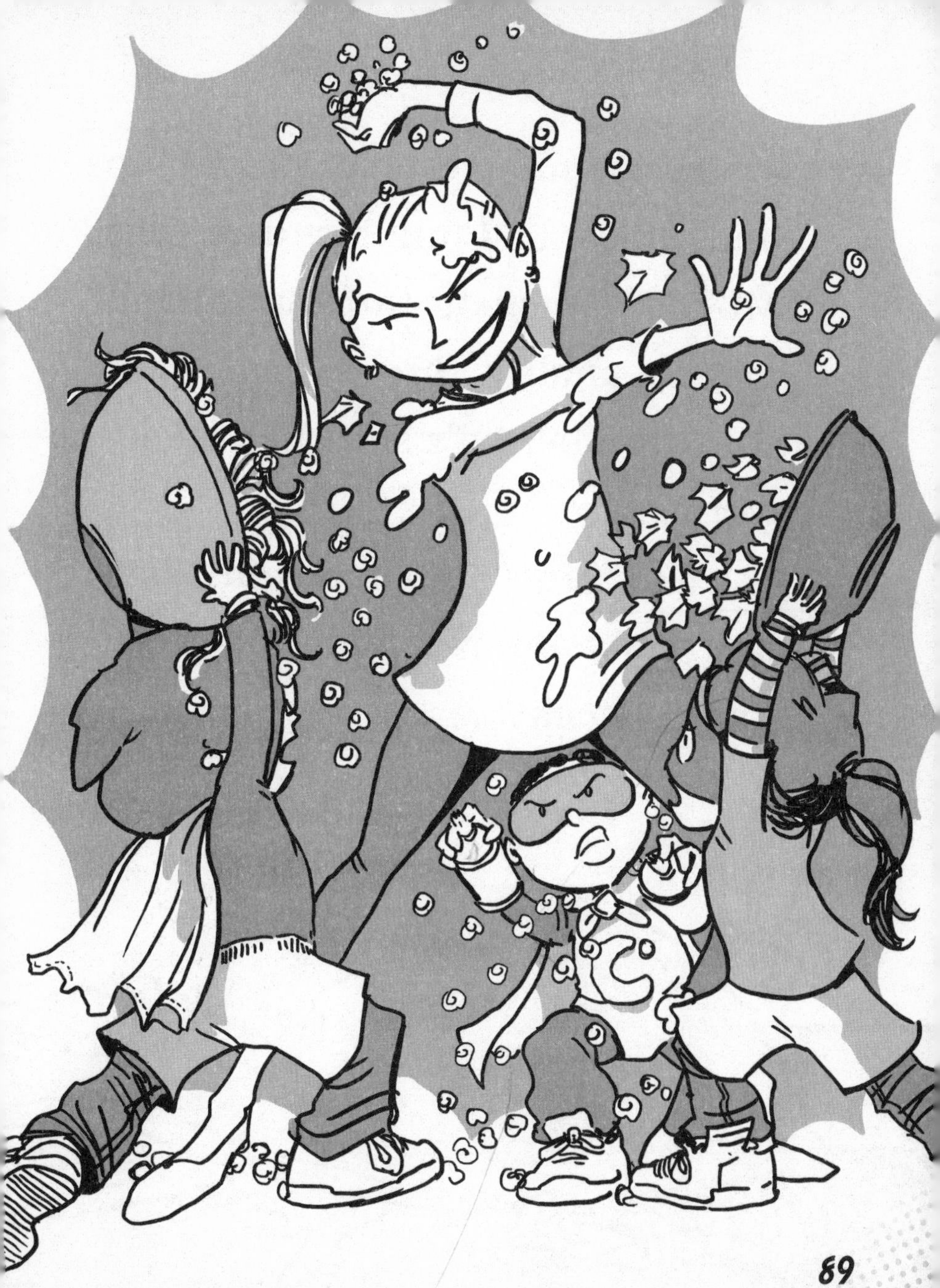

Captain Awesome wound up and unleashed all his awesome MI-TEE spaghetti-throwing might in one mighty throw! The pasta stuck to Melissa's shirt like sticky worms.

"Oh, yeah?" Melissa said. "Well get ready for my Super Popcorn Snow Attack!"

Melissa threw all the popcorn into the air. Popcorn filled the living room! It fell like snow onto Captain Awesome, Supersonic Sal, Nacho Cheese Man, and Melissa.

The three superheroes instantly stopped throwing food and stared in wide-eyed fear at the babysitter.

*She's going to blame us and*

*send the three of us to my room for a billion years!* Captain Awesome thought. *And Supersonic Sal and Nacho Cheese Man don't even live here!*

Melissa popped one last piece

of popcorn into her mouth and looked at Captain Awesome.

*Here it comes.* Captain Awesome braced himself for the super yelling power Melissa was about to unleash, but . . .

**SHOCK!**

Melissa started to *laugh*!

"Is she laughing, or is that some horrible sonic attack?" Nacho Cheese Man whispered to Captain Awesome.

"Oh, man! That was totally awesome!" Melissa said. "I love food fights, and you three are the best!"

## *DOUBLE SHOCK!*

Melissa grabbed a handful of spaghetti from Captain Awesome's pot and plopped it onto her head like a stringy wig. She burst out laughing. And before they knew it, Captain Awesome, Supersonic Sal,

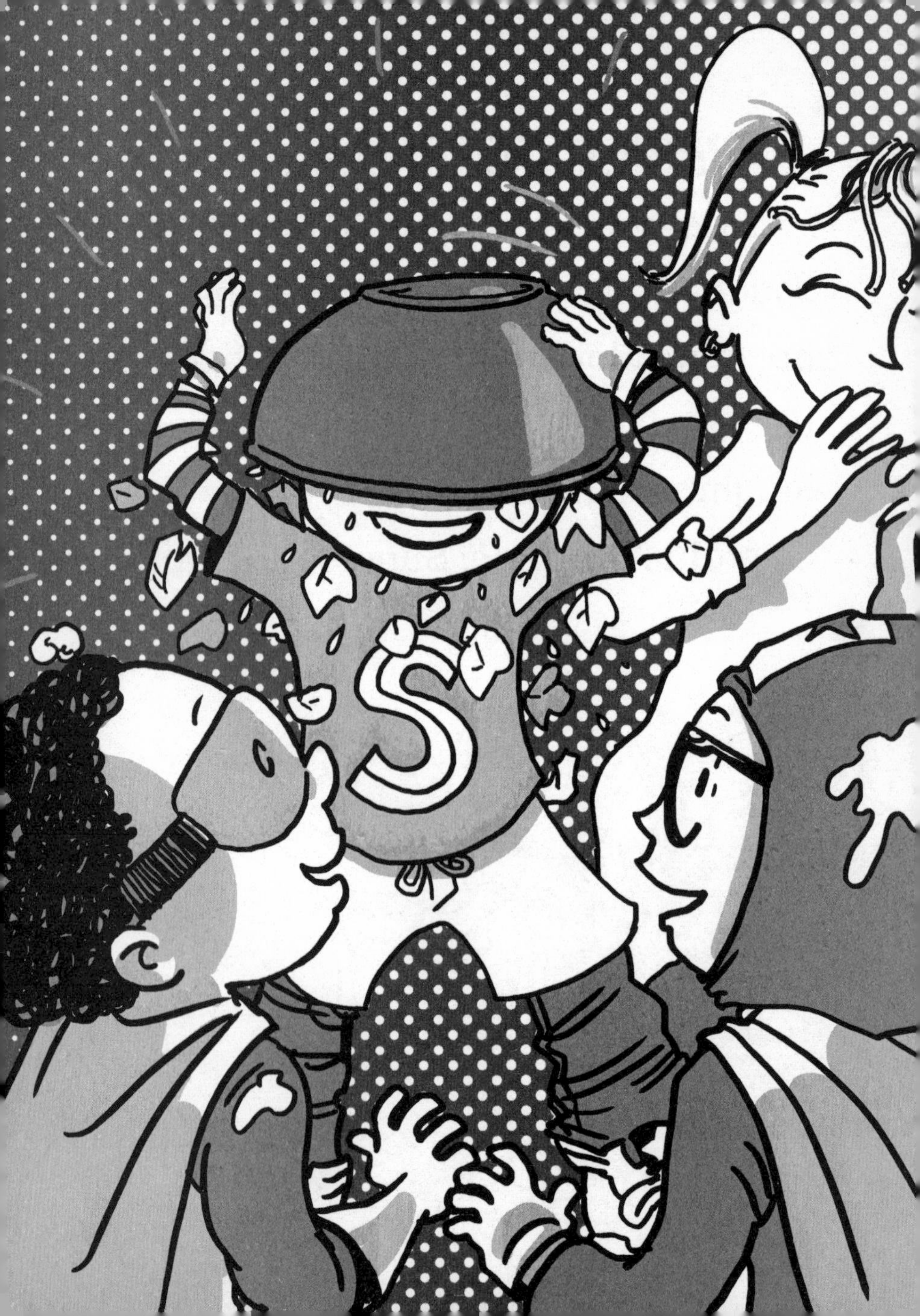

and Nacho Cheese Man were laughing too!

"If this *is* a sonic attack, it's totally working!" Supersonic Sal said, laughing harder than she ever remembered laughing before. Then she dumped the rest of the salad onto her own head.

# CHAPTER 8

# The Joy of Brownies

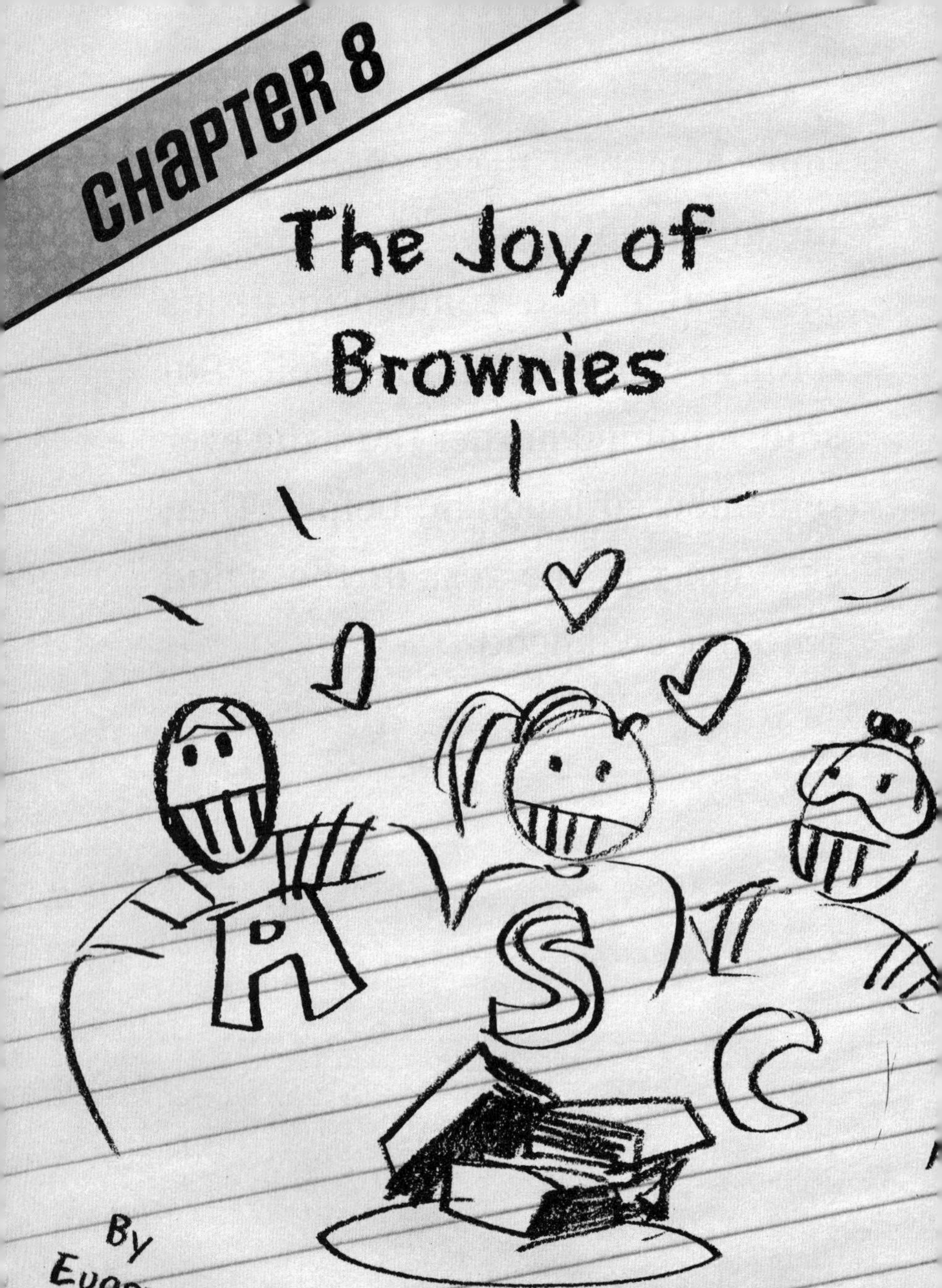

By Eugene

"**M**ees are awthum bownees! Fanks, Mawiffa!" Nacho Cheese Man said—or tried to say—his mouth stuffed with brownies.

"He said, 'These are awesome brownies! Thanks, Melissa.'" Captain Awesome had become an expert at translating Nacho Cheese Man when he talked with his mouth full.

Melissa put a brownie in her

mouth and replied, "Manks, Mafo Meeze Man!"

Everybody laughed, which was quite surprising given that just over an hour ago, they were having a food fight with Eugene's future dinner. But life's funny that way.

Or as Super Dude once said in issue No. 212: "Sometimes you think you know who you should be throwing food at, but if you take a little time to get to know them, you just might realize they're actually pretty cool."

And those wise words never seemed more true than they did now as Captain Awesome, Supersonic Sal, Nacho Cheese Man, Melissa, and even Queen Stinkypants herself sat at the table enjoying some freshly baked brownies—but only after they had cleaned up their foody mess, of course.

"My sister, Meredith, told me that you guys sometimes show up at her school to fight evil, but I never thought I'd get a chance to meet you myself," Melissa said. "This is a real honor."

Captain Awesome's eyebrows shot up. "*You* wanted to meet *us?*" he asked.

"Why, sure," Melissa replied. "It's not every day someone gets to meet real, live superheroes!"

"Sorry for thinking you were a supervillain," Supersonic Sal apologized.

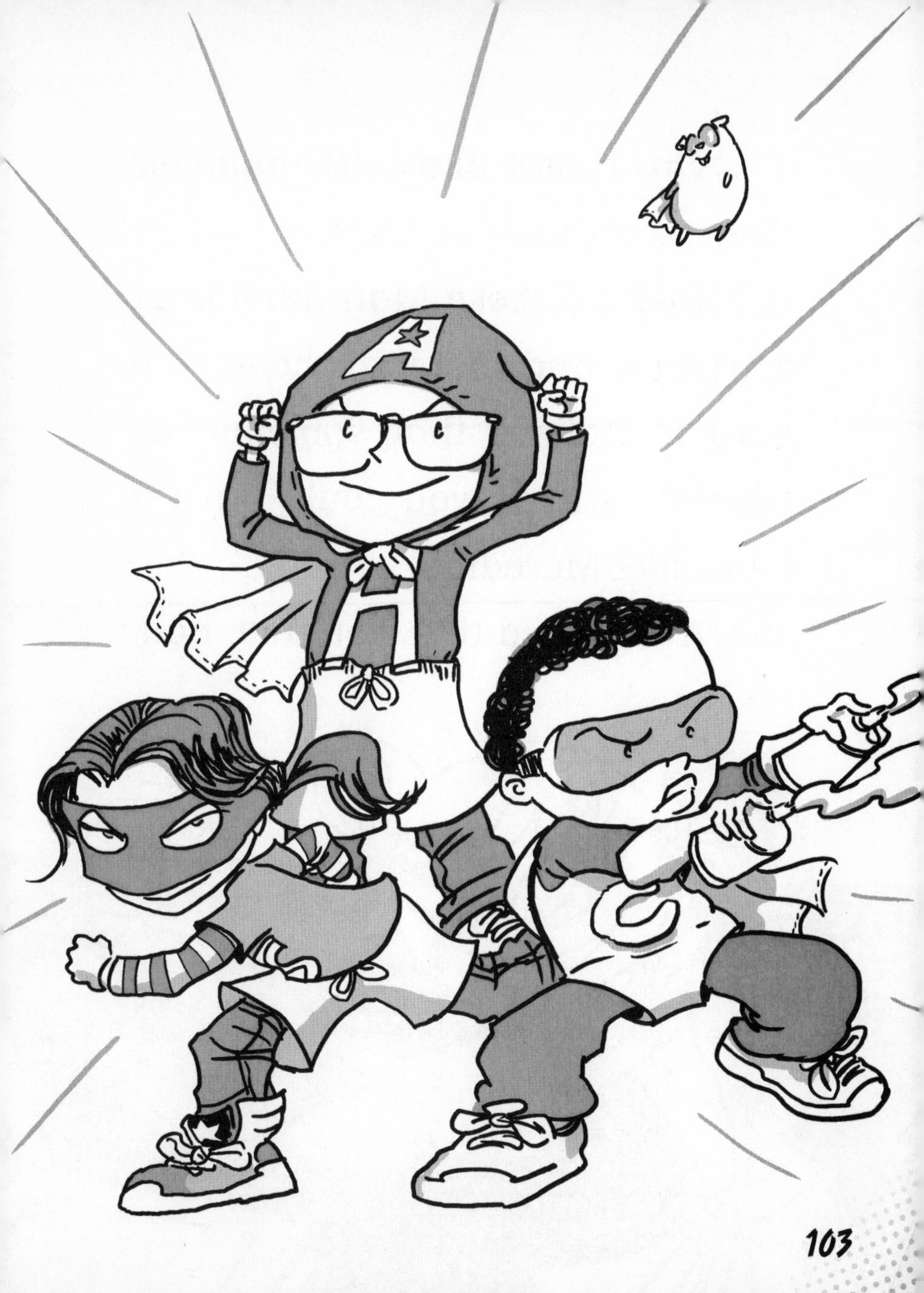

"Oh, that's okay. It happens," Melissa replied.

Nacho Cheese Man nibbled at a brownie and shook his head. "It's hard to believe that someone as cheese-tastic as you could have a sister like Meredith."

"Aw, Meredith's not that bad.

She can be a pain sometimes, but she's really good at making brownies. Actually, my mom helped her make these." Melissa dipped a brownie corner into her glass of milk.

The Sunnyview Superhero Squad stopped mid-bite and looked at their brownies, stunned that something so yummy could come

from someone as evil as Meredith.

Nacho Cheese Man shrugged, ate the final brownie crumbs from his plate, and declared: "Nothing is more evil than wasted brownie!"

It was about time for Nacho Cheese Man and Supersonic Sal to head home.

"Even superheroes have to report to their parents," Supersonic Sal explained as Melissa led them to the front door.

But at that moment, the front door opened on its own. . . .

# CHAPTER 9

# Say Whaaaaaaaaaaaaaat?!

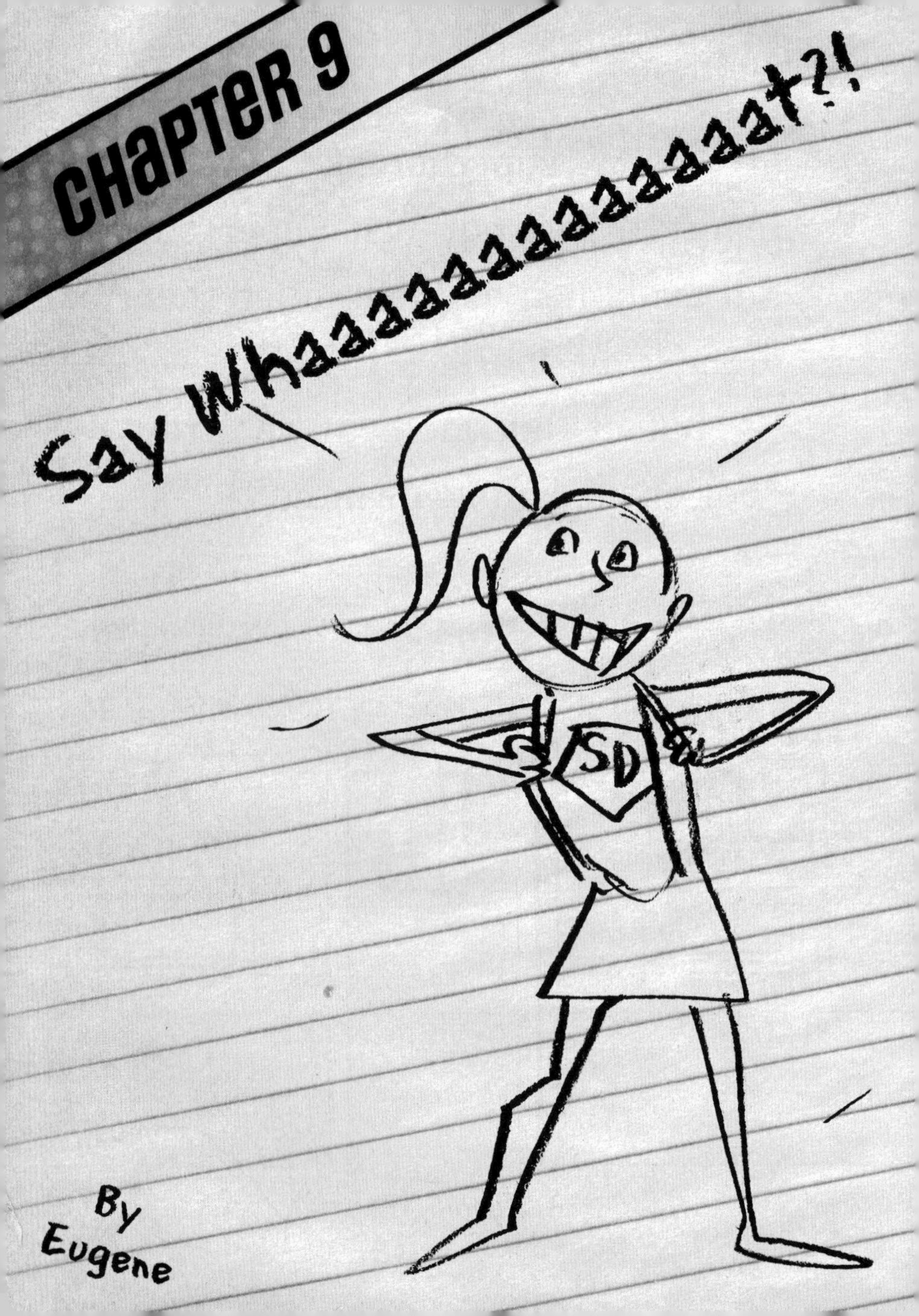

By Eugene

**W**ell, not really. But the front door did open. And behind it were Eugene's parents!

"Mom! Dad! I mean, Mr. and Mrs. McGillicudy! What are you doing home?" Captain Awesome asked.

"The conference was canceled," Eugene's dad said with a sigh. "But on the bright side, our whole weekend's free to spend at home!"

"Oh, Eugene will love that!"

Captain Awesome said, trying to hide the huge grin on his face after hearing the MI-TEE news!

"So, did we miss anything?" Eugene's mom asked.

Captain Awesome, Supersonic

Sal, Nacho Cheese Man, and Melissa shared smiles.

"Nope!" they all said together.

"Come on, guys, I'll walk you home," Melissa said to Supersonic Sal and Nacho Cheese Man.

Melissa put her hand out to Captain Awesome. "It's been great meeting you, Captain Awesome. I'll never forget this day."

"Be good, and good things will happen!" Captain Awesome replied, shaking Melissa's hand.

One shake. Two shakes. Both thumbs up. High five.

Captain Awesome gasped. Did

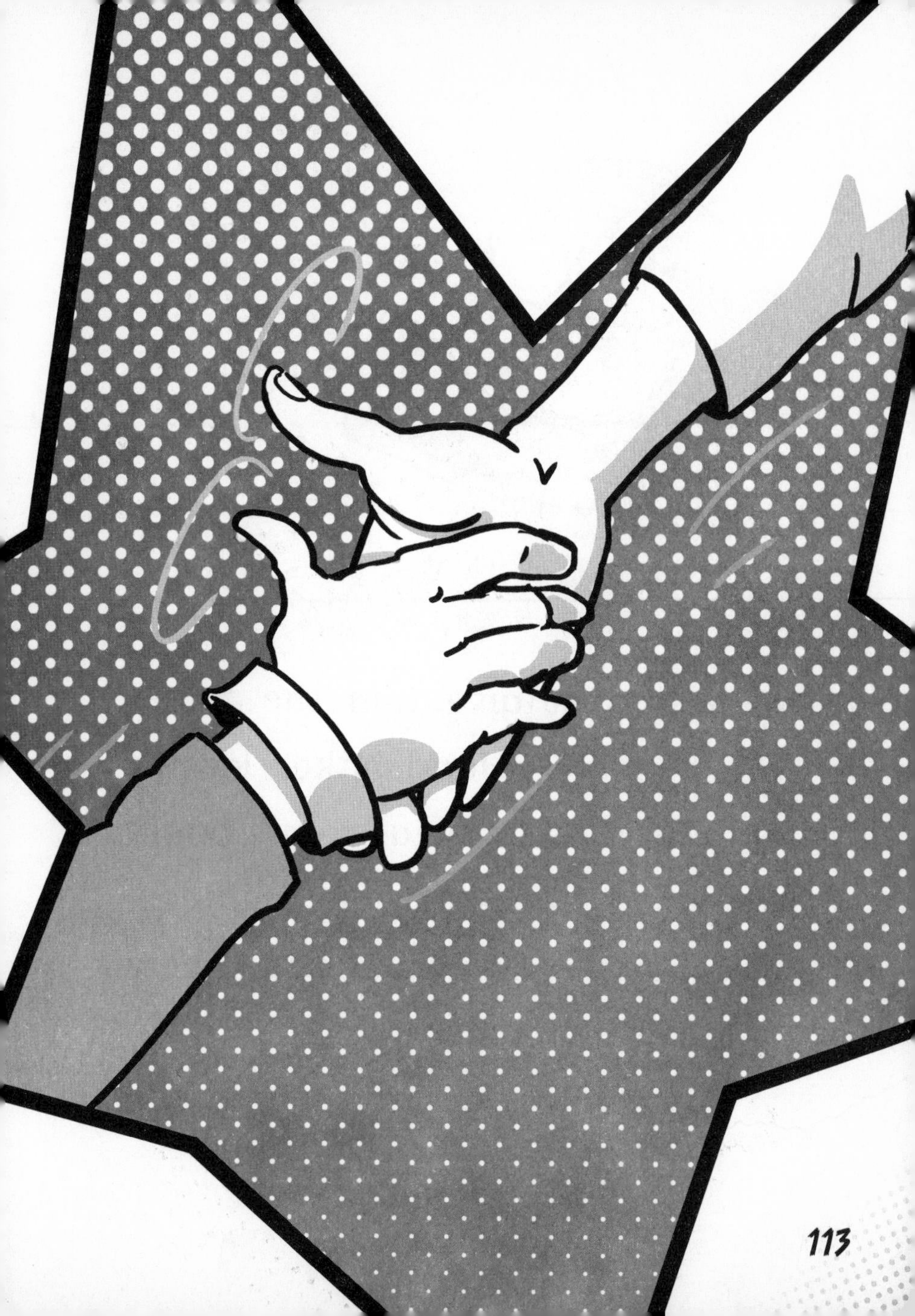

Melissa just give him the Super Dude Secret Handshake, known only by those official comic book-reading, card-carrying, badge-wearing, website-visiting members of the Super Dude fan club?!

Say whaaaaaaaaaaaaaaaaat?!

Melissa was a Super Dude fan?!

Melissa winked and then walked to the sidewalk with Super-sonic Sal and Nacho Cheese Man.

"We should have her babysit again," Eugene's mom said. "She seemed like a very nice girl."

"Oh, she's more than 'nice,'" Captain Awesome replied as he looked at the palm of his hand and smiled. "She's **_MI-TEE!_**"

# THE

END!

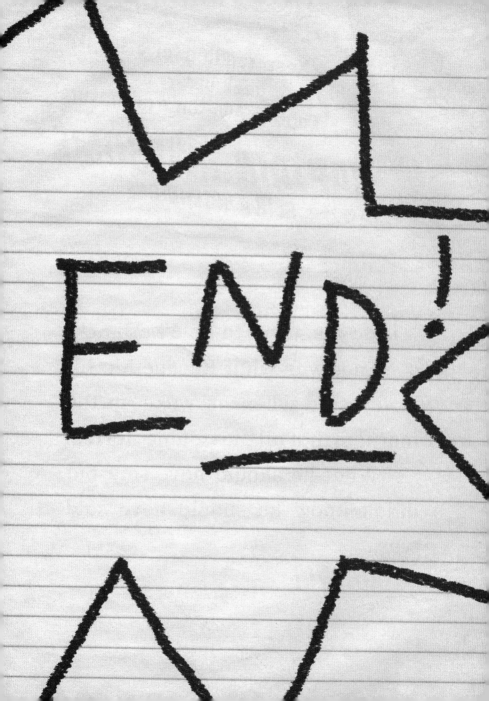

Keep reading for a sneak peek at the next Captain Awesome adventure!

# CAPTAIN AWESOME
## GETS A HOLE-IN-ONE

"**T**oday is going to be awesome!"

That was what Eugene McGillicudy said when he woke up the morning that all the trouble started.

What he should have said but didn't know he should have said was:

**OH, NO!**

It was going to be his worst day ever. But, again, Eugene didn't know that when he woke up.

He didn't even get a hint of his awful day as he walked to Sunnyview Elementary School with his best friends, Charlie Thomas Jones and Sally Williams.

"Smell that fresh air," Eugene said. "This is going to be a great day!"

Charlie nodded. "Let's hurry to class!"

"I don't want to miss even one second of a great day," Sally said.

The trio ran all the way to their classroom.

"Morning, Turbo," Eugene said to the class hamster. Turbo looked up from his carrot and squeaked.

Eugene squeezed his backpack into his cubby and sat at his desk.

His awesome-but-actually-awful day was about to begin.

Eugene's idol, Super Dude, would have sniffed out the evil that was about to strike, but—

Wait, what's that?

You've never heard of Super Dude?

Do you live in a crater on the surface of the dark side of the moon?

How could you not have heard of the greatest superhero in the history of superduperness? Super Dude was the guy who bent back the five fingers of Count Fist-Face and tangled the titanium springs of the bouncy Commander Coil O'Evil.

Super Dude was also the star of the so-real-they-have-to-be-true comic books that made him Eugene's favorite superhero of all time, forever and ever.

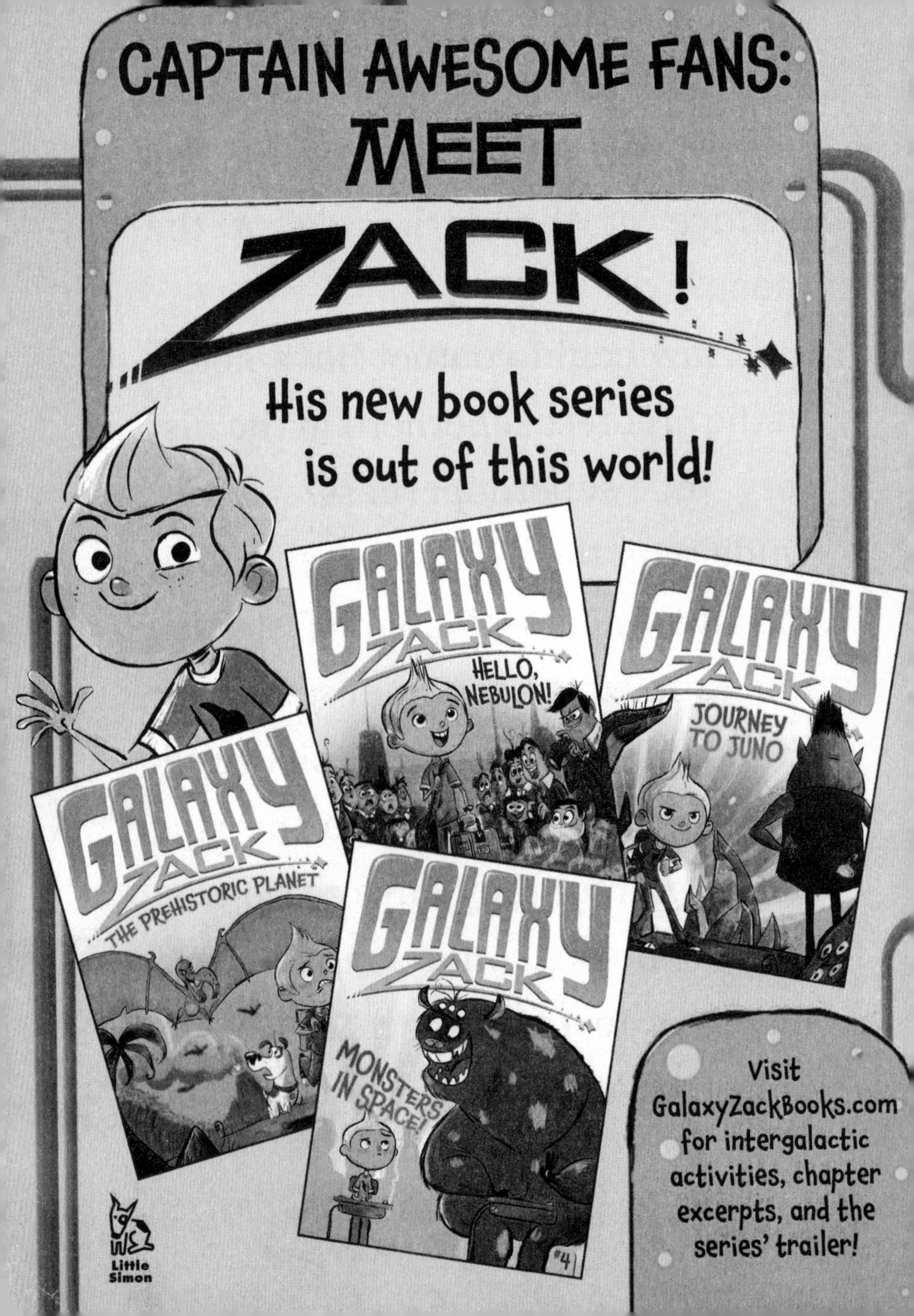

CAPTAIN AWESOME FANS:
MEET
ZACK!
His new book series is out of this world!
GALAXY ZACK
HELLO, NEBULON!
GALAXY ZACK
JOURNEY TO JUNO
GALAXY ZACK
THE PREHISTORIC PLANET
GALAXY ZACK
MONSTERS IN SPACE!
#4
Visit GalaxyZackBooks.com for intergalactic activities, chapter excerpts, and the series' trailer!
Little Simon